BELVEDERE

by GEORGE CRENSHAW

This book belongs to:

A TOM DOHERTY ASSOCIATES BOOK

BELVEDERE

ALL DOGS MUST BE ON LEASH

Copyright © 1974-1981, 1982, Field Enterprises, Inc.

A Tor Book

First printing: July, 1982

ISBN: 523-49020-8

Printed in the United States of America

Distributed by
Pinnacle Books, Inc.
1430 Broadway
New York, N.Y. 10018

"FIRST DOG I EVER SAW WHO NEEDED
SHEET MUSIC TO HOWL AT THE MOON!"

"WHO INVITED HIM ANYWAY?"

" I THOUGHT YOU WERE FOLLOWING ME ! "

" I HEAR THERE ARE LOTS OF STRAY CATS IN THIS PARK. "

" IT'S DIFFERENT ALL RIGHT. BUT IS IT ART ? "

" NOW THAT'S WHAT I CALL A HUNTING DOG. "

" ALWAYS THE COMEDIAN, AREN'T YOU ? "

"NOW WHAT DID I TELL YOU ABOUT CHASING CATS ?"

"HE SIMPLY GOES OUT OF HIS MIND OVER THE *LASSIE* SHOW."

"SURE ENOUGH!...THIS IS THE EXACT SPOT WHERE THE MAP ENDS TOO."

"I WANTED STRONG COFFEE, BUT NOT THAT STRONG."

"TO HECK WITH VISITING HOURS. LET'S JUST RELEASE THE POOCH."

"CANNIBAL!!"

"WHERE'S MY TOSSED SALAD?"

"HELP! HELP! HELP!....ASSUAGE MY APPETITE WITH A CRACKER!"

3-25

"YOU SHOULD NEVER HAVE TOLD HIM ABOUT THE FLOOD OF '07."

3-22

"MOST PROBABLY HIS FRENCH POODLE JILTED HIM AGAIN."

"DON'T BE ANGRY, DEAR. HE'S JUST PRACTICING HIS KARATE."

"HE ALWAYS WEARS THAT RIDICULOUS UNIFORM WHEN I TELL HIM NOT TO LEAVE THE YARD FOR THE DAY."

"YOU LAUGHED WHEN I BOUGHT HIM A FIFTY-FOOT LEASH."

"YOU PUT THE FISH AWAY? GOOD BOY."

"THAT'S *ONE* MOSQUITO THAT WON'T BOTHER US AGAIN!"

"I'LL PLAY MY OWN CARDS IF YOU DON'T MIND."

"QUIET! YOU'LL SCARE THE FISH AWAY!"

" YOU'RE RIGHT. THAT IS BELVEDERE ! "

" HE'S A GREAT LITTLE BIRD DOG. "

"I WISH I HAD HIS CONFIDENCE."

"YOU DON'T SEE MANY DOGHOUSES WITH A WATERBED."

"STARTING MONDAY I'M SENDING YOU *BOTH* TO OBEDIENCE SCHOOL!"

"IT SERVES YOU RIGHT FOR ROCKING SO FAST."

"THIS IS NO TIME TO CONSULT YOUR HOROSCOPE. JUST **SHOOT!**"

"BECAUSE HE WAS A NAUGHTY DOGGIE TODAY, THAT'S WHY."

" NOW WHY DIDN'T YOU THINK OF THAT ? "

"DON'T BELIEVE A WORD HE TELLS YOU. "

"I STILL DON'T THINK THIS WILL GET US BACK TO THE MAINLAND."

"I TOLD YOU NOT TO DETOUR THROUGH THE FOREST."

" WE NEVER CAN GET HIM TO TAKE A BATH AT HOME. "

"WE'VE GOT TO TAKE BELVEDERE OFF VITAMIN PILLS!"

" WOULDN'T IT BE EASIER TO HAVE HIM DRY-CLEANED ? "

" WE'RE ONLY TAKING HIM TO THE KENNEL FOR OVERNIGHT."

"OH, NEVER MIND. I'LL GO TO THE KITCHEN AND GET A MATCH."

"THAT'S JUST HIS LOB SHOT. WAIT'LL HE GETS WARMED UP!"

"THE TROUBLE IS, IF WE TAKE IT HOME, IT'LL BE BRONTOSAURUS FOR BREAKFAST, LUNCH AND DINNER EVERY DAY FOR A MONTH."

" ALL YOU EVER THINK ABOUT IS FOOD ! "

" OH, DON'T PAY ANY ATTENTION. IT'S JUST ANOTHER ONE
OF HIS DOGGIE TRICKS. "

" WITH BELVEDERE AROUND, WE'RE SELDOM BOTHERED WITH SALESMEN."

" I SEE IT BUT I DON'T BELIEVE IT ! "

"WATCH OUT FOR A WHITE SPOTTED POOCH. HE'S TRICKY."

"NOW, IS THAT HOW I TOLD YOU TO PUT THE CAT OUT?"

"NO, I DIDN'T SAY PSSSSST. DID YOU SAY PSSSSST?"

" WHY DID YOU EVER MENTION ETHEL'S HUSBAND WORKS
FOR THE POUND ?!"

" OH, LET HIM PLAY WITH HIS NEW SPACE GUN IF HE WANTS TO."

"OH, GOOD HEAVENS, ORVILLE — WHY NOT LET HIM WATCH FOUR-STAR MOVIE, AND **THEN** CATCH THE SECOND HALF OF THE DOUBLE HEADER?"

"OH, DEAR... I'VE FORGOTTEN WHICH WAS WHICH!"

" I STILL SAY WE'RE SPOILING HIM ! "

" WATCH OUT FOR HIS OVERHEAD SMASH ! "

" WHAT IT ALL BOILS DOWN TO IS, HE WANTS HIS ALLOWANCE INCREASED. "

"BOY, THAT SURE WAS A NOISY CROWD COMING IN LATE LAST NIGHT!"

"HE CALLS A SECRET NUMBER IN LAS VEGAS."

" NO OFFENSE, DOCTOR, BUT I THINK HE WANTS A SECOND OPINION. "

" NOW I'VE SEEN EVERYTHING!"

"THERE'S GOT TO BE AN EASIER WAY TO PULL A TOOTH."

"I DUNNO. I THINK HE LIVES UP THE STREET!"

" HE WASN'T A BIT OF TROUBLE. "

" WOULDN'T IT BE BETTER IF WE JUST CALLED AN EXORCIST? "

" NOW, ISN'T THAT CUTE? WE CAN'T GET HIM
TO TAKE A BATH AT HOME. "

" DO YOU HAVE A CARD FOR AN OBEDIENCE-SCHOOL
TRAINER WHO CRACKED UP ? "

" MAY I MAKE A COMMENT ?... "

" HAVE YOU FOUND A CORK FOR MY FLOAT YET ? "

"WHY DID YOU EVER ASK HIM FOR A LIGHT IN THE FIRST PLACE?"

"YOU CAN ALWAYS TELL WHEN IT'S ABOUT TO SNOW."

"HERE'S GOOD NEWS FROM BELVEDERE'S OBEDIENCE SCHOOL.
HE'S NEARING THE TOP OF THE UNDER-ACHIEVER LIST."

"DON'T LAUGH. HE'S SHOT EVEN PAR EVERY DAY THIS WEEK."

"OKAY, LET'S TRY IT AGAIN ... WHEN I SAY 'TURN ON THE WATER' I DON'T WANT JUST A DRIBBLE!"

"NOW ISN'T THAT CUTE? HE'S TEACHING HIS GIRL FRIEND TO DANCE."

"IT ALL STARTED WITH BEGGING AT THE TABLE."

" YOU'VE GOT TO GIVE THAT POOCH CREDIT FOR
ONE THING, HE THINKS BIG. "

" NEXT TIME, I'LL PACK THE FOOD!!"

" OH, GOOD GRIEF, **JAWS** WAS ONLY A MOVIE. NO REAL
SHARK WOULD EVER ATTACK A BOAT. "

"GO AHEAD, SEE HOW FAR YOU'LL GET!"

"HOW DID I KNOW HE'D TAKE ALL THE CREDIT CARDS."

"NO, NO, NO! I SAID TURN _OVER_ THE BRIDGE!"

"OH, GOOD GRIEF. HERE, LET ME DO THE FLAPJACKS."

"THAT'S QUITE A HUNTING DOG YOU HAVE THERE, ORVILLE."

"COULDN'T YOU ROUGH IT, JUST ONCE IN YOUR LIFE?!"

"I JUST NEED A COUPLE OF ASPIRIN.
NOW WILL YOU CUT THAT OUT?"

"ADMIT IT. YOU'VE BEEN DRINKING AGAIN!"

" I WONDER WHAT KIND OF A FISH STORY THEY'LL TELL THIS TIME ? "

"ALL RIGHT. YOU KNOW THE RULES. ONE FOOT ON THE FLOOR."

"NO, I DON'T WANT TO HEAR A FUNNY JOKE THAT WAS JUST ON THE LATE, LATE SHOW!"

"DOES HE ALWAYS HAVE TO MAKE A GAME OUT OF EVERYTHING?"

"YES, MOTHER, ORV'S BEEN GETTING A LOT OF
USE OUT OF THE TIE."

"I WISH I KNEW HOW BELVEDERE DOES IT. HE NEVER MISSES."

"HE'S SHARPENING MY *WHAT*?!"

"QUITE FRANKLY, SIR, I DON'T THINK THE MANAGEMENT WILL BE HAPPY WITH YOUR CO-SIGNER."

"BETTER WATCH HIM. HE ASKED FOR A MENU."

"WE MADE A DEAL. BELVEDERE PROMISED TO MOW THE LAWN IF I AGREED TO TRIM THE EDGES."

"IT'S THE ONLY WAY WE CAN GET HIM TO TAKE A BATH."

"THEY'VE HAD ONE FOR THE ROAD, ONE FOR THE STREET AND ONE FOR THE FREEWAY. NOW THEY'RE TOASTING THE BACK ALLEY."

"GET READY, I THINK IT'S WORKING!"

"ADMIT IT! YOU'VE BEEN HANGING AROUND THAT MUSEUM AGAIN, HAVEN'T YOU?!"

" OH, COME NOW... I DON'T LOOK *THAT* BIG IN MY STRETCH-PANTS !"

"ALL I DID WAS INVITE THEM OUT BACK TO MEET BELVEDERE."

"HIS RECORD IS 3/10 OF A SECOND."

"HAS ANYONE SEEN MY ROLLING PIN?"

"I THINK WE WINGED HIM."

" YOU'VE GOT TO HAND IT TO THE A.S.P.C.A.---
THEY NEVER GIVE UP TRYING. "

"IT'S SORT OF WHAT YOU'D CALL A *POOCH PAD.*"

" JUST ONCE, I'D THINK HE COULD ROUGH IT. "

" I THINK HE'S TRYING TO TELL YOU SOMETHING, DEAR. "

"NOW, ISN'T THIS BETTER THAN A NIGHT OUT WITH THE BOYS?"

"LET'S NOT TRY **THAT** AGAIN!"

" HE LOVES A GOOD BUFFALO HUNT. "

"OH, OH! LOOKS LIKE WE LEFT THE T.V. ON ALL NIGHT!"

"I BELIEVE HIS FRIEND IS AN ENGLISH SPANIEL."

" HE'S A GREAT LITTLE FIGHTER. "

" OKAY, OKAY, OKAY! IT'S UNCLOGGED! "

"ON THE OTHER HAND, MAYBE **WE'RE** STANDING ON THE CEILING."

"WE SHOULD HAVE KNOWN BETTER THAN TO GIVE HIM AN INDOOR TRAMPOLINE FOR HIS BIRTHDAY."

"I STILL SAY, IF YOU WERE ANY KIND OF TRUE SPORTSMAN, YOU'D HAVE GONE ON YOUR TRIP IN SPITE OF THE RAIN."

"WHEN I WANT YOUR OPINION, I'LL ASK FOR IT."

"I SHOULD HAVE KNOWN BETTER THAN TO ASK YOU FOR HELP."

"WHAT ELSE DOES HE DO?"

"WHERE THE HELL DO YOU GO EVERY DAY?"

"ALL RIGHT, I'M WAITING. DO YOUR MAGIC TRICK."

10-26

" ARE YOU TWO FEUDING AGAIN ? "

10-27

" OH, WHAT IS IT ? "

"I SAW THIS MOVIE LAST WEEK. THE BUTLER DID IT!"

"HAIL, EARTH PEOPLE. GREETINGS FROM THE PLANET..."

"THAT WON'T SCARE OFF PEDDLERS AND YOU KNOW IT."

"WHAT DO YOU MEAN, 'OKAY, **NOW** I'M READY'?!"

" NOW I'VE SEEN EVERYTHING ! "

" SAY, BERNIE, DO WE HAVE A BUSINESS DOG'S LUNCH ? "

" IF HE COULD ONLY SWIM. "

" I SHOULD HAVE KNOWN BETTER THAN TO LET YOU DRIVE. "

"VERY GOOD. NOW, WHAT'S YOUR OPINION ON FOREIGN AID?"

"FOR A FREE BEER, HE'LL LISTEN TO ANYONE'S TROUBLES."

"GIRAFFE SHOTS ARE NOT LEGAL."

"NOW, IS THAT HOW I TOLD YOU TO TENDERIZE THE STEAK?"

" ...AND THIS WILL BE BELVEDERE'S ROOM. "

"THERE GO HIS THIRD SET OF CONTACT LENSES THIS WEEK."

"THEY'RE PRACTICALLY INSEPARABLE."

" HE'S REALLY QUITE A GOOD LITTLE WATCH DOG. "

" I THINK WE'RE GETTING INTO PYGMY COUNTRY. "

" I KNEW **SOMEONE** WOULD FIND US ! "

" HE'S COME UP WITH THE PERFECT ANSWER TO THE HOT WEATHER PROBLEM. "

" I WAS JUST WONDERING, MILDRED, WHY HIS FOOD IS 100% BEEF, AND OUR HAMBURGER IS 25% SOYBEANS. "

"JUST SPEAK RIGHT UP IF I BOTHER YOU IN ANY WAY."

"NOW WHERE DID HE GO? I WANTED HIM TO SEE THIS."

" NOW THAT'S WHAT I CALL A HANGOVER!"

"ADMIT IT. YOU'RE MAD AT ME ABOUT SOMETHING, AREN'T YOU?"

"WHY DID YOU EVER ASK HIM TO SHARPEN THE PICTURE?"

"WHO TURNED ON THAT FAN?!"

" HIS BOWLING AVERAGE IS WAY DOWN. "

" DID YOU HEAR A TWIG SNAP ? "

"HE'S IN ONE OF HIS MORE INSPIRED MOODS TODAY."

"COME BACK!...WE PROMISE WE'LL BE GOOD."

"SHHHH. HE'S TRICKY."

"THOUGHT I HAD HIM CORNERED THERE FOR A MINUTE."

" ON MY `LOOKING FOR OWNER OF LOST DOG' AD
WOULD YOU PLEASE ADD THE WORD **HELP!?** "

" YES, NOW THAT YOU MENTION IT—
WE DO HAVE A CAT AND A DOG."

" HEY! EASY WITH THAT QUICK GROW ! "

" NICE BREAK. "

"CHIEF, I'D LIKE TO REPORT THE TRICKIEST POOCH I HAVE EVER ENCOUNTERED!"

"OH, GOOD GRIEF. LET HIM KEEP HIS NEW PET IF HE WANTS TO."

"IF IT'S **ANY** KIND OF BIRD, HE'LL FLUSH IT OUT!"

"BEWARE OF HOT DOG PACKING PLANTS."

" ORVILLE, YOU'VE USED TOO MUCH DETERGENT. "

" I ALWAYS KNEW HIS BIRD IMITATIONS WOULD PAY OFF."

"DON'T GO, OLD FRIEND!...WE PROMISE NOT TO MIX OATMEAL IN YOUR HAMBURGER AGAIN."

"OH ALL RIGHT. I'LL FEED YOU!"

"HE'D BE A GREAT RETRIEVER...IF HE COULD ONLY SWIM."

"THEY'RE ALL GOOD. BELVEDERE TESTED EVERY ONE."

" YOU KNOW HE DOESN'T TAKE CALLS DURING PRIME-TIME VIEWING HOURS. "

" YESSIR, THAT WAS A **BIG** DUCK YEAR. "

"IT'S BEEN A PLEASANT EVENING. I FOUND YOUR VIEWS ON FOREIGN POLICY MOST ENLIGHTENING AND I'M SO GLAD YOU APPROVE OF INTRA-FIDUCIARY SOLIDARITY."

"SO **THAT'S** WHERE HE'S BEEN SPENDING HIS AFTERNOONS."

"SURE I KNOW HIM. THAT'S HALF NELSON HIMSELF."

" WANNA DRAG ? "

" I THINK HE WANTS IN. "

"AND JUST WHAT MAKES YOU THINK THIS HAIR-GROW CONCOCTION OF YOURS WILL WORK?"

"IF HE'D JUST BARK OR BITE, I'D KNOW HOW TO HANDLE HIM."

" YOU SHOULD NEVER HAVE ASKED HIM TO SPEAK. "

" COLOR THE THIRD EYE GREEN. "

"GO AHEAD, ASK HIM TO PLAY DEAD."

"NOW, DON'T CRITICIZE HIM, DEAR. WE NEED THE FISH."

"WELL, YOU ALWAYS WANTED TO BE THE CENTER OF ATTRACTION."

"BEST LITTLE OL' GUIDE-DOG A MAN EVER HAD!"

"HE JUST READ MAN IS THE HIGHEST FORM OF LIFE."

"HE'S MISSING THE WHOLE IDEA OF SPEED READING."

"NOW SEE HERE — YOU PROMISED NO SHORT CUTS!"

"WOULD YOU READ ME THAT WEATHER REPORT AGAIN?"

" WELL, WHO WON THE BIG POKER GAME? "

" EXPECTING SOME GOOD SHOWS TONIGHT? "

" YOU DON'T SEE MANY DOGHOUSES WITH ADJOINING BATH. "

" NOW, IS THAT HOW I TOLD YOU TO SHOE A HORSE ? "

"I DON'T CARE IF HE DID HAVE A BAD DAY AT OBEDIENCE SCHOOL. I'LL DO ALL THE AFTER-HOURS *UNWINDING* AROUND HERE."

"OH, FOR PITY'S SAKE. LET HIM PLAY WITH YOUR TEETH. YOU'RE NOT EATING ANYTHING."

" IT'S A LADY GODIVA RIDING HABIT. "

" LOWEST TIDE I'VE SEEN IN YEARS. "

" THAT'LL TEACH YOU TO CHASE AFTER A FARM BALER! "

" WHY DID I EVER MAKE THAT ELECTION BET ? "

" SORT OF A NIFTY MANEUVER, IF I DO SAY SO MYSELF. "

" HE'S GETTING PRETTY GOOD AT THAT BANK SHOT!"

" HE'LL DO ANYTHING JUST TO ATTRACT ATTENTION."

" THE NEW MAILMAN MUST HAVE HEARD ABOUT YOU. "

" IT'S HARD TO BELIEVE THEY MET IN THE PEACE CORPS. "

" BELVEDERE IS READY WHENEVER YOU ARE, DEAR. "

" ALWAYS THE CLOWN, AREN'T YOU ?! "

"GOOD HEAVENS, NOT SO LOUD. YOU'LL STARTLE MRS. SMITH."

"ALL I ASKED WAS, WOULD HE TAKE A PICTURE OF US TOGETHER?"

"YOU CAN ALWAYS TELL A DOG THAT HAS A LICENSE."

"BELVEDERE JUST LOVES HIS NEW HAMMER."

" HEY, COME BACK HERE ! "

" WHY DO I EVER ASK HIM TO HELP WITH ANYTHING ? "

" YOU GOT THE WHEEL OFF ALREADY ? GOOD BOY ! "

"JUST A MINUTE THERE, BUSTER!"

"I SAID, JUST THE PERCH!"

"JUST WHAT DID YOU WRITE ON THAT NOTE IN THE BOTTLE?"

"IN THESE WATERS WE'LL FIND PLENTY OF......SWORDFISH."

" THE CALL OF THE WILD JUST ISN'T WHAT IT USED TO BE. "

"I DUNNO... I NEVER SAW HIM BEFORE EITHER!"

"WHAT CAN I DO? HE'S REGISTERED RIGHT HERE."

"YOU DIDN'T PUT THE FORK ON THE LEFT."

"GUESS IT JUST ISN'T OUR DAY, OLD BUDDY."

"WOW! THE WATER POLLUTION IS WORSE THAN I THOUGHT."

"NO GAMES TONIGHT. DADDY'S TIRED."

" BETTER KEEP AN EYE ON THAT NEW WAITER. "

" NOW! I HOPE YOU'RE HAPPY! "

" FOUR IRON. "

" NOW THAT'S WHAT I CALL A CARROT CAKE ! "

"I'M AFRAID TO ASK HIM WHERE HE GOT THEM!"

"HE GETS MORE OUT OF A BOOK THAN ANYONE I KNOW."

"I HAD THE MOST AWFUL NIGHTMARE LAST NIGHT."

" EASY ON THOSE BUMPS, PARTNER ! "

"LOOKS LIKE FINNEGIN LOST AGAIN."

"VERY FUNNY!"